Samuel French Acting Edi

MW00623070

Women Laughing Alone With Salad

by Sheila Callaghan

SAMUELFRENCH.COM   SAMUELFRENCH.CO.UK

FOR PRODUCTION ENQUIRIES

UNITED STATES AND CANADA
Info@SamuelFrench.com
1-866-598-8449

UNITED KINGDOM AND EUROPE
Plays@SamuelFrench.co.uk
020-7255-4302

Each title is subject to availability from Samuel French, depending upon country of performance. Please be aware that *WOMEN LAUGHING ALONE WITH SALAD* may not be licensed by Samuel French in your territory. Professional and amateur producers should contact the nearest Samuel French office or licensing partner to verify availability.

MUSIC USE NOTE

IMPORTANT BILLING AND CREDIT REQUIREMENTS

WOMEN LAUGHING ALONE WITH SALAD was developed in part in Center Theatre Group's Writers Workshop, premiering at the Kirk Douglas Theatre in Culver City, California on March 6, 2016. The performance was directed by Neel Keller, with projection design by Keith Skretch, choreography by Ken Roht, scenic design by Keith Mitchell, costume design by Ann Closs-Farley, lighting design by Elizabeth Harper, and sound design by John Zalewski. The cast was as follows:

GUY .... David Clayton Rogers

SANDY ....Lisa Banes

MEREDITH ....Dinora Z. Walcott

TORI .... Nora Kirkpatrick

CHARACTERS

TORI – (20–25) Impossibly slim. Also plays **JOE**.

SANDY – (late 50s) An Upper East Side grande dame. Also plays **GUY** (Act Two).

MEREDITH – (30–35) Slightly larger build, wears some sort of retro fifties outfit with postmodern touches. Rockabilly-type. Also plays **BRUCE**.

GUY – (late 20s) Cute, scrubby. Also plays **ALICE**.

AUTHOR'S NOTES

Note for the actor who plays Guy in Act One:

This character is largely inactive throughout most of the act, which makes him tricky to play. He receives his catharsis in the second act, so it's important not to complete his arc in Act One. Consequently, it's advisable to play him against his lines to some degree, so his confusion has room to become increasingly more destabilizing. While his lines suggest he is rude, superficial, self-absorbed, and whiny, he is also sexy, charming, charismatic, funny, sly, affectionate, and very good at making his terrible qualities seem attractive. This contributes to his central dilemma: he wants all the women in the play to love him as he slowly becomes aware he doesn't understand them.

Note for all the actors:

While the characters function in an archetypical fashion and the dialogue is stylized, the conversations should still feel like attempts at real communication, perhaps without the realization that it has not been achieved.

ACT ONE

Part One: The Park

(Lights up on three women [the women who play **TORI**, **SANDY**, *and* **MEREDITH***] of varying ages sitting in a park. They all have huge bowls of salad and forks.)*

(A nearby lit bus stop sign has a picture of a woman laughing alone with salad and the slogan "She's Waiting for You. HotMatch.com, the Only Dating Site You'll Ever Need.")

(They eat their salad like it's the most delicious and hilarious thing ever. It goes on for a while. They eat, glance at each other in acknowledgment, laugh, eat, play with cherry tomatoes, etc. It is just so much frivolity. The woman who plays **SANDY** *eventually becomes full. She laughs her way offstage.)*

(The remaining two women eventually become skittish, suspicious, catty, possessive. You're looking at my salad? Don't covet my cucumber. That kind of thing.)

(Meanwhile, a **GUY** *enters with a burrito. Sits next to them. They freeze, salad halfway to their mouths. Their eyes watch his burrito. He unwraps it with excruciating slowness. The women are rapt.)*

*(***GUY*** gets a text. Reads it.)*

GUY. You gotta be kidding.

(Notices the salad chicks. Huh. That's weird. He moves away and they disappear, carrying their precious salad bowls with them.)

*(**GUY** dials. Listens. As he lingers…)*

Part Two: The Beauty Counter

*(**SANDY** appears at the cosmetics counter of a very high-end department store. She wears a tastefully lux ensemble. Speaks to an unknown saleslady.)*

*(**SANDY**'s phone rings. She checks the caller. Decides not to answer. Smells/tests creams and potions.)*

GUY. *(Into the phone.)* ...Okay maybe you're on a work call or getting a facial or whatever, maybe that's why you sent me to voicemail...or, maybe you just don't wanna talk to me 'cause you'd rather send commands from on high and expect me to comply without further question...and I told myself I wasn't gonna leave a message 'cause you never listen to them anyway...but here I am. So.

I got your text. And here's my answer. No. I'm not going across town to Zabar's buying your priest boyfriend his Bavarian chocolate espresso rum cake again. You can buy it yourself. I'm tired of it. I'm not your employee. I'm the wet fleshy blob you expelled from your vagina twenty-nine years ago, and I don't appreciate being manipulated. I have a life. A job. I mean both kind of suck right now, but they're still mine.

Also dinner this week sounds great. Looking forward to it.

Also. I can't hang up. Because I know that the second I do, I'm gonna walk to the liquor store, plop down my credit card, and buy your priest boyfriend his Bavarian chocolate espresso rum cake again. Because I'm dead inside. Ha!

Love you bye.

*(He hangs up and vanishes as **SANDY** hits her Bluetooth headset.)*

SANDY. ...And this is for the hands? Is it new? Great. I'll take it.

Call Kristen.

Hi Kristen it's Sandy, when you get a chance would you call my son and remind him to pick up the monsignor's chocolate Bavarian cake? I texted him but I'm too busy to follow up. Also he hates when I ask him to do things. Thanks. Okay listen I'm stuck in traffic and not gonna be able to make lunch with Barb so could you reschedule and maybe order me a salad from down the street? Red wine vinegar, cranberries, celery, four black olives, cucumber slices, cooked broccoli, some red onions, mushrooms, and sliced almonds. Oh, I forgot to ask if Jeremy from Singer Properties called. Great, what did he say.

(She gestures to the saleslady to wrap up one of the creams for her.)

Uh-huh. Uh-huh. Great. Perfect.

(As she listens, something wet, fleshy, blob-like, and glistening with blood drops from between her legs and lands on the floor with a splat.)

Shoot.

*(**SANDY** regards it in horror but not surprise – obviously this has happened before, more than once.)*

Okay Kristen listen I'll have to call you back.

(She hangs up. Regards the blob. Looks around to see if anyone saw.)

(She scoops the blob up and tucks it back between her legs. It stays. She looks vaguely relieved.)

Part Three: The Television

(A TV commercial is projected. Women laugh alone with salad in slow motion.)*

(Slowly, beneath this, a woman's voice, gentle and bright.)

FEMALE VOICE 1 (SANDY). Making healthy choices. Taking care of me. Feeling good. Living good. Healthy and clean. I like that. For me. Because I matter. Loving myself because someone has to. Loving me for living good and eating good. Loving myself. Must. Or at least should. Possibly could if I eat salad. But only salad. Must do what. People tell me. Instead of living. The life I could live. I eat salad. So I'm healthy. Therefore I must be happy. But deep inside. Somehow I'm not. Must eat more salad.

FEMALE VOICE 2 (MEREDITH). Possible side effects of laughing alone with salad include nausea, heart palpitations, dizziness while standing, temporary night blindness and compulsive gambling.

FEMALE VOICE 3 (TORI). Can we get a "women laughing alone with salad while wearing white and doing cartwheels during their periods" what-what? Hey. I love my lifestyle. And my tank tops. And yogurt. Boo-yah! Suck it.

(Product: Freetex Brand Feminine Hygiene Products.)

---

*A license to produce *Women Laughing Alone With Salad* does not include performance usage rights for any commercials. Licensees should create their own.

Part Four: Rooftop Bar

*(Swanky lounge. Music.** **MEREDITH** *walks over to the bar to get a drink. Notices* **GUY**.*)*

MEREDITH. Ha! He's looking at me again. Saw me dancing downstairs. Six years of jazz, two of tap, two months of ballet before the teacher told me I was too fat to be in the Christmas show. Also gymnastics. I probably should lead with that, right?

GUY. Caught me staring again. Heh. Seems to like it. That's cool. Bet she took gymnastics as a kid. She's super flexible probably. Why are flexible chicks so hot? Fun to bang a chick with her knee behind her ear. Especially a bombshell like that. Meat on her bones. Yeah. She could smother me with her maternal bosom.

MEREDITH. I don't want to be a slut and get naked the second we go back to your place, but well I kind of do. I just don't want you to think it's my idea. Why isn't he moving? He could be a freak show. I don't mind, I just want to make sure I know what I'm getting myself into.

*(***MEREDITH*** *pulls a subtle, sexy dance move seemingly aimed at* ***GUY***.*)*

GUY. Whoa. You see that shit? Ha. That was for me. I see you. I see you. I bet you're a little slutty. Bet you'd get naked the second we got back to your place. But then act like it was my idea. I dig that.

MEREDITH. I can tell him about the time I was in Berlin at that club and that guy told me he was a producer for a TV show where kids dance and he asked if I would go on it, and I was too high to believe him so I just kept laughing. If I tell him that he'll think I'm someone worth sleeping with. Or maybe he'll think I'm

---

*A license to produce *Women Laughing Alone With Salad* does not include a performance license for any third-party or copyrighted music. Licensees should create an original composition or use music in the public domain. For further information, please see Music Use Note on page 3.

desperate. Well I'm both. I can be both, right? Should I go over?

GUY. She seems worldly. I bet she has stories. I bet she's been to Berlin. Clubbing around Europe. Yeah. You're wild. You're audacious. My mouth is dry. What am I getting into here? Nothing bro, you're just looking. Like you always do. You wouldn't even know what to do with that. She would yank you out of time and DESTROY YOUR WORLD. Go home, pussy. Go! Either go home, or walk over to her and be the sick bratty rude foul motherfucker she wants you to be.

> (*Beat.*)

Jesus... Okay. Shit.

> (**GUY** *starts moving toward* **MEREDITH** *almost involuntarily, as if being pulled by a magnet.*)

Keep it together, man.

> (**MEREDITH** *is there.*)

Hi.

MEREDITH. Hi.

GUY. I saw you dancing.

MEREDITH. I saw you see me. One time I was at this big club in Berlin in this converted power plant and this guy came over to me and told me he was a producer for a TV show where kids dance and he asked if I would go on it.

GUY. Cool.

MEREDITH. I'm a really good dancer. I took tap and ballet as a kid. And gymnastics. I can put my knee behind my ear.

GUY. Yay.

MEREDITH. What about you?

GUY. I've never been to Berlin. But I'm flexible for a guy. I can do the splits.

MEREDITH. Like right now?

GUY. Only when I'm super drunk and jamming out pretty hard.

MEREDITH. Are you in a band?

GUY. Karaoke.

MEREDITH. You look like you're in a band.

GUY. So does every other asshole in here. I like your style. You're like retro. Like a pin-up.

MEREDITH. *(Re: her chest.)* It's my bullet bra.

GUY. Yeah. How many tattoos?

MEREDITH. A bunch.

GUY. Got a favorite?

MEREDITH. The one on the back of my shoulder. It says "Forever Fierce." It actually says "Forver." The dude misspelled it. But I thought it was so funny I left it. I also have a secret tattoo.

GUY. Where?

MEREDITH. On my lower lip. Inside.

GUY. Can I see it?

(**MEREDITH** *pulls down her lower lip.*)

"Bite me." That's great. It's got like double meaning.

MEREDITH. Do you? Have tattoos?

GUY. I have a skull right above my pubic bone.

MEREDITH. Because your dick is poison?

GUY. Because I'm an idiot. I did it when I was fifteen. But I don't regret it. It's kind of like, I dunno. A body diary.

MEREDITH. Yeaahhh... Cool.

GUY. Are you drunk?

MEREDITH. A little.

GUY. You seem a little drunk.

MEREDITH. I should have had more than just salad for lunch.

GUY. You're not a salad-eater.

MEREDITH. Did you know there are more lingerie shops in Paris than bakeries? It's 'cause French girls see themselves as beautiful BECAUSE of their physical

flaws, not in spite of them. Paris in the twenties, man…
Those bitches *owned* their shit.

GUY. I like you. I like the way you talk. I like the way you
dress. I like the way you smell.

MEREDITH. I like the way you like that stuff about me. I also
like the way you flirt.

GUY. I don't really try to flirt. I just don't generally talk to
girls I'm not interested in sleeping with.

MEREDITH. This conversation just got twenty percent more
interesting.

GUY. Only twenty?

MEREDITH. Needs room to rise. Like a cake.

GUY. I like girls who love cake.

MEREDITH. Guys like girls who love salad. The internet told
me.

GUY. Fuck the internet.

MEREDITH. Are *you* drunk?

GUY. Yeah.

MEREDITH. What are you drinking about?

GUY. Right now? You.

MEREDITH. Ha!

GUY. I've been trying to get the courage to come talk to you.

MEREDITH. I'm not *that* scary.

GUY. You're scarier than you think, Meredith.

      (Beat.)

MEREDITH. I didn't tell you my name.

GUY. You didn't have to.

MEREDITH. Okay.

      (Beat.)

Now what?

GUY. I wanna say some dirty dirty shit to you.

MEREDITH. Okay.

GUY. Where should I start?

MEREDITH. My mouth. Tell me what you think of it.

GUY. I picture it wrapped around my cock.

MEREDITH. Wow. What about my wrists.

GUY. I hold you down by them while I nail you face down in your bad little place.

MEREDITH. Damn. We got there fast.

GUY. You don't like to waste time.

MEREDITH. Neither do you.

GUY. So let's go.

MEREDITH. Where?

GUY. In the bathroom.

MEREDITH. Yeah?

GUY. In the alley.

MEREDITH. Yeah?

GUY. In the basement.

MEREDITH. Yeah?

GUY. On the surface of the sun.

MEREDITH. Yeah.

GUY. Now.

MEREDITH. No.

GUY. When?

MEREDITH. Later. I need to yank you out of time first. BANG.

> *(Music changes. They are in twenties Paris. Couples jazz-step drunkenly, drink moonshine, etc.* **MEREDITH** *and* **GUY** *start dancing.)*

We're in Paris now. 1920. Everything is so decadent. The drinks are decadent. The music is decadent. Are you decadent?

GUY. Well, I called my mom once when I was getting a blowjob from a prostitute, so...

MEREDITH. Spectacular. And what's your mom like?

GUY. She used to be an activist.

MEREDITH. All right. What is she now.

GUY. A cunt.

MEREDITH. Ha! I remind you of her, don't I.

GUY. Yeah, kind of.

MEREDITH. In what way?

GUY. Because you don't seem to care what I think of you. Because you probably have a higher tolerance for pain than me. Because you're probably smarter than me. Than *I*.

MEREDITH. You wanna fuck your mother.

GUY. Not literally, but sometimes, yeah. Like, rage-fuck. Like, fuck you for asking my dad to leave. Or fuck you for getting older and obsessing about your looks. Or fuck you for making me love horseback riding and snowboarding.

MEREDITH. You're rich?

GUY. Maybe.

MEREDITH. This night is great. This is a great night. Like the air is moist and heavy and filled with adventure and I'm gonna grab a plastic knife and cut myself a slice.

GUY. Devil's food.

> (**MEREDITH** *unstraps a flask from her garter, takes a belt, and hands it to* **GUY**. *He also takes a belt.*)

> (**GUY** *screws on the cap and tucks the flask slowly into her garter. His hand remains on her thigh. Her breath catches.*)

MEREDITH. Now.

GUY. Where.

MEREDITH. Close.

GUY. Bathroom, alley, basement, sun.

MEREDITH. Carpet.

GUY. Whose?

MEREDITH. Yours.

GUY. Um okay. I have to ask the girl I'm with.

MEREDITH. Oh. She's here?

GUY. I told her not to come, but...

MEREDITH. Is she skinny?

GUY. Yeah.

MEREDITH. Like how skinny?

GUY. Like so skinny people worry about her.

MEREDITH. Is she so skinny I could shove her entire body up my ass without any lube?

GUY. You want to shove my girlfriend up your ass.

MEREDITH. YES I DO, OKAY? Because I'm tired of pretending to be something I'm not. Civilized. Don't make me civilized, Person-Whose-Name-I-Don't-Know-Yet. I don't want to be your girlfriend. I want to go down on your girlfriend while you watch. I want to make her come harder and louder than you ever could. I want you to fear me, and I want her to fear you fearing me. I want to lead with my mass, I want the gravity of my circumference to suck you and everyone you love into me, and I want you to stick there against my body like a suction cup.

GUY. This is literally my greatest dream and my worst nightmare.

> (**TORI** *appears. She sips a drink forlornly in the corner.*)

That's her.

MEREDITH. Oh my god.

GUY. I don't even know if I'm in love with her. I mean I enjoy being adored. I have empathy for her, but I don't really have the other thing. The step *after* empathy.

MEREDITH. What's that?

GUY. Like that moment of self-annihilation when you kind of become the other person? I dunno. There's something wrong with me.

MEREDITH. You're right. There is.

> (*She starts to walk away.*)

GUY. Hey.

MEREDITH. You brought her here to watch you hit on another chick.

GUY. That doesn't mean I don't respect her.

MEREDITH. I wonder if she'd agree with you on that. Should we ask her?

GUY. No.

MEREDITH. The thing about dudes who go around with chicks like that? They need *props.* Pretty little trinkets to prove what MEN they are. When in actuality? It's the total opposite. THEY ARE BABIES. Why don't you grow the hell up and be a man.

(*Beat as* **GUY** *processes this. It hurt.*)

Ah. So *that's* the sound of someone's balls shrinking. Paris a bit much for you? Too decadent?

GUY. I don't even know why we're here.

MEREDITH. I was romanticizing a time when the feminine ideal was vital and autonomous.

GUY. You know what I think?

I think you know as well as I do that none of this is happening.

(*Music stops, we're back in modern-time.*)

You come here alone, like you do most Friday nights, thinking you'll find some dickhead drunk enough to go home with you, but not too drunk to lose his erection. If he even gets one in the first place. Which rarely happens. Except tonight, when you see me across the room watching you dance. We make small talk and it's super hot. But then you take me to metaphoric Paris. And you say some mean stuff that makes me nervous. And I say some mean stuff back and walk away.

And then, I'll probably get really drunk very quickly and pass out in the cab ride back to my apartment while my skinny lady-friend gives me head in the back seat. And I will try to forget about this encounter completely. Except the part where I accidentally brush up against your breasts and think to myself, this chick has a gorgeous rack. And maybe I'll picture myself sucking on your nipple for a split second. But that's it.

MEREDITH. That's not a nice thought. Let's go backwards a few beats. Let's go back to the part where you tell me you like watching me dance.

GUY. I was just looking at your ass. Like every other guy here.

MEREDITH. That's a start...

GUY. You have a rip in the back of your dress. Right at the crack.

> (**MEREDITH** *checks. Sure enough, there's a gaping hole showing off her cotton panties.*)
>
> (**GUY** *exits. A large bowl of salad falls from the sky. Then a large fork.* **MEREDITH** *catches it with glee and joyfulness.*)
>
> (*Glowing mightily behind/above/around her is an ad with a woman laughing alone with salad and the slogan "Handleman's Lite Dressing. For the YOU in You."*)
>
> (**MEREDITH** *dances the "dance of the seven lettuces" in the glow of the ad. Romaine. Frisée. Iceberg. Arugula. Butter. Oak leaf. Baby spinach. It is quick and exuberant. She exits.*)
>
> (**GUY** *emerges. He has been lurking. He saw the dance. He doesn't know what to make of it. But this chick is definitely under his skin.*)

Part Five: The Carpet

(GUY is passed out on the couch. TORI enters, overly bright.)

TORI. You drank a lot last night. You're never this hungover. It's weird. It's supposed to get to like, seventy-five today. Spring! Yay. Pink toenails and pastel tank tops. Midnight fro-yo. Riding our bikes around the city like gangstas. Ha! Makes me feel, like, powerful? You know? Like I own something in the world? I dunno.

(GUY appraises TORI oddly. Something has changed...)

What?

GUY. You're pretty.

TORI. Thanks. You want brunch? We could go get brunch.

GUY. Sure.

TORI. There's that place on Avenue B. The one that Kenyatta and his girlfriend always want us to try. They have buckwheat soba pancakes with tofu cream cheese. They also have like fried sesame rice balls and kimchi burritos. It's like generic Asian-fusion or whatever. His girlfriend eats like a caveman but she's a coke-head so all the fat just melts right off her. They use organic soy sauce. They have dim sum too.

GUY. Okay.

(He continues to watch her oddly. She senses it but barrels ahead as though things are normal.)

TORI. I'm so OVER the winters here. Even with all this body fat I freeze to death. You know if we lived in LA we'd have an orange tree and I'd squeeze my own orange juice with like a manual press. And I'd wear flip flops every day. Even in the rain. And do yoga, like *serious* yoga, like I'd get my certification. I think I could get my dad to pay for that, right? He paid for my tuition and my Vespa. I think he still feels guilty about my stepbrother molesting me. Isn't that weird? I barely remember it, but yet I get tons of free shit for the rest of my life.

(Beat. She looks at him staring at her.)

What? Seriously.

*(**GUY** shrugs.)*

They have normal food there too. Like bacon and eggs and toast. Should I put on NPR?

GUY. No.

TORI. Okay.

GUY. You smell like puke.

TORI. I brushed my teeth.

GUY. Brush your *tongue*.

TORI. Sorry.

*(She goes to brush her tongue. **GUY** starts getting dressed.)*

(Nonchalant.) Who was that fat chick you were hitting on all night?

GUY. She wasn't fat.

TORI. Well-marbled.

GUY. She had beautiful breasts.

TORI. Are you *trying* to make me feel insecure?

GUY. She was the only gal there who looked like she was having a good time.

TORI. *I* was having a good time. *You* didn't notice.

GUY. I was avoiding you. Because when I say stuff like "I need space" you show up to the club anyway.

TORI. Maybe if you stopped pelting me with clichés you'd get better results.

GUY. Maybe if you stopped *being* a cliché I wouldn't need space...

TORI. You're cute. Don't you have a tweet to write? About being a young feller in the big bad city with an ulcer and a creative writing degree whose meeeeaan girlfriend won't let him do anal?

GUY. You let me do anal. Twice.

TORI. Complete accident. Both times. I was too drunk to employ corrective measures.

    (Beat.)

GUY. God. That kind of changes everything.

TORI. Really?

GUY. Kinda. Makes me feel like, rapey.

TORI. Well it was, a little. But like, fun rapey, not like sex-offender rapey.

GUY. But you didn't enjoy it.

TORI. I didn't *despise* it. It's just not my thing.

GUY. *Twice.*

TORI. What's the big deal?

GUY. If I didn't like something you were doing I would tell you to stop.

TORI. But part of you *wanted* me to like it.

GUY. Because some girls do! And you're a little kooky, which is what I dig about you, and I wanna do kooky shit to you that you like, but it's messed up to act like you like something when you think I *want* you to like it but you don't *actually* like it.

    (Beat.)

TORI. I'm sorry I let you ass-rape me. It won't happen again –

GUY. And like, how you bring up the fact that you were molested like it's all, "Oh, I was just waiting for the bus and I got finger-banged by my brother!"

TORI. *Step*-brother. What does that have to do with ass-rape?

GUY. And how you memorize the entire menu at every goddamn place we go eat but then you order a leaf of lettuce?? EVERY SINGLE TIME?

TORI. I have food allergies, what is your point?

    (Beat.)

GUY. Nothing.

    I just wish…

    I wish you could be more like, audacious or something. Whatever.

    (Beat.)

TORI. You know, I've been getting checked out *way* more recently. By older men especially. Like, as someone who's had periods in her life of feeling totally invisible? It actually feels really good. It's like a little sex fairy sprinkled some magic dust on me and for like a teeny tiny second I have power.

    *(Lights change. **GUY** freezes.)*

    (A boastful, aggressive, punk-ish rap song begins to blast. It's really loud, and masculine, and maybe kind of sexist. **MEREDITH** and **SANDY** emerge from nowhere dressed like old-school Fly Girls. They cradle riches in their arms and approach **TORI** and lip-synch back-up vocals. **TORI** mouths the main lyrics to the song, channeling a very powerful male rap singer. She is the absolute opposite of what we would expect. She lip-synchs some braggadocio rhyming lyrics about how she is getting rich, banging bitches, and taunting critics/haters. The women deliver **TORI** a scepter, a robe/cape, riches, and a crown while she struts and preens. **GUY** is just a prop in this, an object, a trophy. **TORI** works the crowd/audience. It's thrilling. On the strength of a strident vocal attack,*

---

*A license to produce *Women Laughing Alone With Salad* does not include a performance license for any third-party or copyrighted music. Licensees should create an original composition or use music in the public domain. For further information, please see Music Use Note on page 3.

an urgent, stomping percussion, and a serpentine show-stopping electric guitar, the song builds to an adrenaline-fueled climax. Then...the other two women disappear. **GUY** *unfreezes and* **TORI** *wiggles in between his legs. She takes a hit of his joint. Beat.)*

GUY. Let's go to Paris.

TORI. Why?

GUY. Why not?

TORI. Um...okay but. I wanna go to LA.

GUY. Everyone goes to LA. LA *acts* like a sexy place but Paris is the real deal.

TORI. Except everything there is drenched in butter.

GUY. So what?

TORI. *Dairy.* I'd starve.

GUY. You could take those lactard pills.

TORI. Ew.

GUY. Come on. Let's be decadent. Just for once. You never do that.

TORI. Yes I do.

GUY. When was the last time you were decadent?

TORI. I was decadent last night. In the cab. When I *swallowed your load.*

GUY. That doesn't make you decadent. It's only decadent if you like doing it! And you know it makes me uncomfortable when you use porn verbage.

TORI. "*Verbiage.*" Asshole.

(*Beat.*)

(*Lighter.*) Whatever. Let's just order something from that horrible diner you love. The one that smells like old people. You can get the hangover special. With extra sausage gravy and bacon from a wild boar.

GUY. What about you?

(*Small beat.*)

TORI. Um.

GUY. What're you gonna order?

    (Long beat.)

To eat?

TORI. Um.

Anything.

Um.

Eggs benedict.

Um.

Belgian waffle.

Um.

Steel-cut oatmeal.

Um.

Applewood smoked bacon.

Um.

Puff pastry. Um.

Greek omelet.

Um.

Um.

Um.

Iced donut.

Um.

Poppy seed bagel.

Um.

Turkey sausage.

Um.

Corned beef hash.

Um.

Um.

Um.

Smoked salmon.

Um.

Um.

Um.

Um.

Um.

Um.

Um.

Um.

Tofu scramble.

Um.

Ham croissant.

Um.

BLT.

Um.

Country biscuit.

Um.

Breakfast burrito.

Um.

Um um um um um um umumumumumumum French toast.

French fucking toast.

GUY. You'll eat French toast.

TORI. Every last bite. I'll eat it. I'll pour goddamn syrup on it and slather it in butter and I'll cut huge triangles with my tiny plastic knife and I'll chew it all up and I won't even gag.

GUY. Won't even gag.

TORI. I won't. And I'll look at you on your balcony in your thrifted shirt with your stupid hair blowing back even though there's no wind and I will eat the goddamn entire serving of French goddamn toast out of a Styrofoam container with a plastic fucking fork.

(Long beat.)

GUY. Except you won't.

Because you never.

Do.

(Beat.)

GUY. I should get going anyway. I need to be at work by noon.

TORI. It's not even ten –

GUY. See ya.

> (**GUY** *kisses her on the head and exits.* **TORI** *remains behind. Curls her knees into her body. Rocks a little.*)

TORI. *(A whisper.)* What's my name?
What's my name?

Part Six: The Restaurant

*(Lights up on **GUY**, miserable. Staring at his apron. Beat. He dons it. Fixes his hair. Gets ready for the worst job on the planet.)*

GUY. Okay.

(He heads off to the kitchen.)

(Three anonymous women sit alone at separate tables, forks and knives in hand, waiting. Lunch rush. A bell rings.)

*(**GUY** rushes in with a tray. On the tray is a plate with a red pepper. He delivers it to the woman who plays **MEREDITH**.)*

Okay here we have a forty-six calorie vegetable with a side of braised nothing. Enjoy.

(The woman proceeds to cut up the pepper very, very slowly into tiny pieces and eat slow-mo. She is in utter ecstasy.)

*(Bell rings, **GUY** delivers a plate carrying one yellow pepper to the woman who plays **TORI**.)*

Okay a locally grown dirt object pulled from the soil and triple washed. Delish.

(The woman rubs the pepper on her cheeks and gums very slowly. She laughs quietly to herself.)

*(Bell. **GUY** delivers an onion on a plate to the woman who plays **SANDY**, who licks her chops and rubs her hands together.)*

*(**GUY** cuts the onion for her. Pleasant. She smiles.)*

This is an onion. It's just a fucking onion. You ordered an onion from a fancy restaurant. Eat it.

*(She eats a piece. **GUY** watches them as they all eat in ecstatic slow-mo. He gets on a mic.*

He speaks in a deep, slow, smooth-jazz voice.
Perhaps some R&B or slow-jam hip-hop
plays.)

GUY. Mmmmmmmmmm.

Right.

Yum yum.

Yummy.

Oooooooh.

Uh-huh.

Yeah.

Eat it.

Make it happen, ladies.

Work.

Now you got it.

Go baby.

Bring it down.

Mmmm-mmm.

Keep me waitin'.

Eaaaaasy does it.

Melt in your mouth.

Shawty you feel me.

Don't fight it.

Don't hide it.

Just ride it.

Begging for it.

On your knees.

To the beat.

Eating won't quit.

Jackpot baby.

Hmmmm.

Mmmm.

Mmmm-mmm-mmm-mmm-mmm-mmm-mmm-
mmm-mmm-mmm-mmm.

*(The women finish. Sighs of contentment and relief. Dab their mouths with napkins. Lean back in their chairs. **GUY** clears their plates.)*

(Beat.)

*(The woman who plays **TORI** slides her finger down her throat and hurls.)*

Part Seven: Upper East Side

(**SANDY** *sits on a chair with her hands immersed in a large bucket. She struggles to drink a glass of water through a long, long straw.*)

(*Out her window: A building with a gym on the second floor. Sign in the window has a woman struggling to drink water and the slogan "Fit 4 Less! 0% Down for the Month of June!"*)

(**GUY** *appears, places the cake box on the table, kisses his mom.*)

SANDY. You made it!

GUY. I always make it. You look stunning. As usual.

SANDY. Thank you baby. How'd the cake come out?

(*He shows her.*)

Perfect. The monsignor will be thrilled.

(*She notices his pallor.*)

You look like you got hit by a train. How's the restaurant?

GUY. I quit.

SANDY. No. When?

GUY. Today. All those coiffed ladies with shiny hair refusing to order a decent meal... Also they just added like seven new salads to the menu. Memorizing all that new shit, it's like I was studying for the GREs again.

SANDY. As if you actually studied.

GUY. Fuck grad school. Did Kerouac go to grad school? Did Hemingway?

SANDY. Someday you're gonna wish you studied something practical as a fallback.

GUY. Like what?

SANDY. Marketing.

GUY. Only cowards and losers go into marketing. I'll find some other shitty job.

SANDY. You know you don't have to...

(*Beat.*)

GUY. Did you get my message yesterday?

SANDY. Yes.

GUY. Did you listen to it?

SANDY. No. I've been busy.

GUY. What are you doing?

SANDY. This nutty Mediterranean treatment. Supposed to take years off your hands.

GUY. Botox stop working?

SANDY. It's *new*. For the *hands*. Hands are the true marker of a woman's age –

GUY. Come on, I'm starving. You're not even dressed.

SANDY. I think maybe I'm gonna stay home, honey.

GUY. Whattaya mean, I just took two trains and a cab to get here. I've been looking forward to a sloppy lasagna all week.

SANDY. I'm in the middle of my treatment. If I stop now I'll have to start all over again.

GUY. How long does it take?

SANDY. Four to five days.

GUY. How long you been sitting there?

SANDY. Since midnight.

(**GUY** *finally peers into the bucket. He is a little surprised.* **SANDY** *laughs.*)

They won't hurt you. They never leave the bucket.

GUY. What are they doing?

SANDY. Feeding. They eat all the dead skin off your hands and then some. It doesn't hurt.

GUY. But...your fingers...

SANDY. What about them?

GUY. Where are they?

SANDY. They ate them, honey. I wasn't using them anyway. I never cook anymore, I've forgotten how to drive, I use voice-recognition on my phone...honestly they were a distraction more than anything.

GUY. Mom, that's idiotic.

SANDY. No more idiotic than the hundred other things I've done to my body to keep it fresh and vigorous.

GUY. Get up.

SANDY. Also my uterus keeps falling out. I'm better off sitting.

> (*He picks up his phone. Presses a button.* **SANDY** *mouths her salad order in sync with* **GUY** *– they've done this before.*)

GUY. Hey, yeah, delivery, I'd like a sloppy lasagna and a side of meatballs, a liter of Coke, a can of Diet Coke, and a side of greens with red wine vinegar, cranberries, celery, four black olives, cucumber slices, cooked broccoli, some red onions, mushrooms, and sliced almonds. Forty-one East Eighty-sixth Street apartment 12b. Thanks.

> (**GUY** *pulls out a cigarette.*)

SANDY. Don't smoke in here.

GUY. You let the monsignor smoke indoors.

SANDY. I'm gonna ask an elderly priest with lupus to hobble himself to the elevator every time he wants a cigarette?

GUY. YES!

SANDY. You're acting like a jealous lover.

GUY. You spend more time with him than with me.

SANDY. He lives in the building.

GUY. Okay.

> (**SANDY** *leans in confidentially, smiling.*)

SANDY. So tell me. What's going on with you and that girl? The one with the pronounced clavicle?

GUY. Tori.

SAND. I like her. Why don't you get serious about her?

GUY. She wants us to move to LA.

SANDY. Interested?

GUY. It's too far.

SANDY. From what?

> *(Beat.)*

From me? Aw honey.

GUY. Whatever.

> *(Tiny beat.)*

(Slightly shy.) Also. I met this other chick. At a club. So.

SANDY. What's this one like?

GUY. Confident. Um. Audacious. And god, her smell...

SANDY. What does she look like?

GUY. She's kind of like a pin-up. Retro hairdo...

SANDY. Uh-huh...

GUY. She wore a, she called it a bullet bra...

SANDY. I had one of those in the eighties! Go on.

GUY. Worldy...she's been to Berlin...

SANDY. Well-traveled. Wonderful. What else?

GUY. Ah...she's...ample.

> *(Beat.)*

SANDY. How ample?

GUY. 'Bout yay big?

> *(He gestures with his hands.)*

SANDY. Oh dear.

GUY. What?

SANDY. Honey.

GUY. What if she's my future?

> *(Sound of another loud-ish chomp. **SANDY** jumps, peers into the bucket.)*

SANDY. Yikes! There goes my left thumb. Sayonara, sucker... heh heh.

GUY. Great.

SANDY. Look. I want you to be happy. But I just don't see you with a bigger girl.

    *(Beat as **SANDY** appraises **GUY** carefully.)*

Something's on your mind. I can tell.

    *(**GUY** says nothing.)*

Something you can't talk to me about?

GUY. I don't know. Yeah.

SANDY. Why not try?

    (Longish beat.)

    *(**GUY** lights up his cigarette. She lets him.)*

GUY. Okay fine.

You um.

Like a month before you kicked Dad out.

Um you, your assistant, Brian?

SANDY. Yes.

GUY. Um.

I knew he was in love with you of course, everyone was, but I sensed something else, and it was confirmed when I...saw, um, one night, it was like three a.m., I got up to get a glass of water, he was going down on you in the kitchen, you had your back pressed against the sink and he was on his knees beneath your nightgown, I recognized his Converse high tops, at first I thought he was adjusting your hem, but I watched long enough to see you come, which was horrible, and then I went back to bed and jerked off, which was equally horrible.

God, I should stop. I should stop talking.

SANDY. No, please.

Go on.

GUY. Um.

And um like the next week he was organizing some files in your office while you were at work, and I walked in and closed the door behind me and he was like hey dude, what's up, and I held out a baggie of coke and asked him to blow me.

(*Beat.*)

SANDY. Did he?

GUY. Yeah.

SANDY. Where?

GUY. On my penis.

SANDY. You know what I / mean.

GUY. On your stepladder. I sat on the high rung with my pants at my ankles.

SANDY. Did he snort the coke?

GUY. *That's* what you want to know?

SANDY. He was a clean kid. I'd be surprised.

GUY. Yeah, he snorted it.

SANDY. Then what?

GUY. We did a few key hits together.

SANDY. And then?

GUY. I blew him. I wasn't good at it. He kept telling me to go slower, to grab his hips. Then he told me he had to finish working, so I left the room and brushed my teeth and went to school.

SANDY. And you're telling me this because…

GUY. I don't know –

SANDY. Okay. Okay. You're working some stuff out. That's great. That's great. Are you seeing Dr. Rosenbaum again, honey? Because I really think you should / be discussing some of this with –

GUY. I also had sex with some assistants you *weren't* fucking.

(*Beat.*)

SANDY. Who?

GUY. Elisabeth. Kerry. Kristen.

SANDY. You slept with *Kristen*?? She's so tacky!

GUY. See, this is why I didn't tell you! You have all these, like, *opinions*…

SANDY. Am I not supposed to? Why don't you just tell me how I should / feel.

GUY. Why did I have to get a blowjob from the dude you were banging? Why has that girl from the club been in *every dream* I've had for the past three nights? And why am I so goddamned ashamed of it?

SANDY. How would I know?

GUY. Because I think you might be the reason.

SANDY. You're blaming *me* for your inability to come to terms with the things you want?

GUY. Isn't that why you had to slut around behind Dad's back? Because you couldn't come to terms with the things YOU wanted?

SANDY. *(Savage.)* Don't you dare act like you know anything about my marriage.

GUY. Don't you dare act like you were anything more than a whore.

> *(Suddenly, a loud chomp echoes in the room.* **SANDY** *screams in pain.)*

SANDY. AAARRRRGGGHHHHHH!

> *(This echoes forever and much larger than it should.* **GUY** *freezes, unhearing.)*

> *(Lights change.)*

> *(***SANDY** *and* **GUY** *are now out of time.* **SANDY** *pulls from the bucket an enormous slice of angel's food cake with vanilla frosting. Her hands are bloody and her fingers are stumps. She begins to eat the cake without utensils, just her face.)*

> *(***GUY** *throws on a necktie and a fake moustache.)*

GUY. You're so good with the baby, honey.

SANDY. Thank you.

GUY. You're a natural.

SANDY. I am.

GUY. He resembles you more than me.

SANDY. He does.

GUY. You look terrific with all that extra weight on you.

SANDY. I do.

GUY. I'll bet it's nice not to have to worry about your waistline anymore.

SANDY. Sure is.

GUY. Nice to dissolve like a cube of sugar into the warm, milky tea of motherhood.

SANDY. Absolutely.

GUY. You were getting tired of the protests anyway.

SANDY. I was.

GUY. Tired of being cooped up for hours in a smelly car with ten angry lesbians on their periods...

SANDY. True.

GUY. Tired of screaming your throat raw about what you believe your gender deserves.

SANDY. I was.

GUY. Of making yourself ugly and unappealing while at the same time demanding respect.

SANDY. Completely.

GUY. It's not natural.

SANDY. It isn't.

GUY. You were meant to lose your looks at thirty.

SANDY. I was.

GUY. Along with your feminine power.

SANDY. Indeed.

GUY. As I become more distinguished and formidable and robust with age.

SANDY. It's true.

GUY. Now you can "have it all."

SANDY. I can.

GUY. A baby you adore, a clan of mommy friends who aren't intimidated by you...

SANDY. Yes.

GUY. A part-time job when you're ready for it, to make you feel relevant...

SANDY. Yes.

GUY. AND...a husband who feels safe with you here, all swaddled in your maternal envelope.

SANDY. Finally.

GUY. You are an amazing woman. With your big breasts leaking milk and your gut all floppy like a freezer bag.

SANDY. I made the choice to stay home with my baby. It's my right. As a woman.

GUY. Women's rights. It's what you've been fighting for all along.

SANDY. How about that!

GUY. Now I must go fornicate with the next young thing who bends provocatively over my wastebasket.

SANDY. Go fuck yourself.

GUY. What?

SANDY. Love you honey.

GUY. You too.

> (**GUY** *removes the moustache and the tie, freezes.*)
>
> (*The cake returns to the bucket.*)
>
> (*Lights change back.*)

SANDY. I made a family. Dream come true. Not one regret.

GUY. You hate angel's food –

SANDY. Give me a hand?

> (**GUY** *grabs a towel or napkin and helps clean the cake from his mother's face.*)

GUY. You didn't have to marry him.

SANDY. What was the alternative?

GUY. You coulda raised me with the lesbians or whatever. Stuck me in a papoose and marched me on Washington...

> (**SANDY** *regards him incredulously.*)

I don't mean literally. But like. If I'd been surrounded by all that stuff as a kid...maybe I'd be a little less fucked up.

(Beat.)

SANDY. If I'd remained an activist and not married your father...

GUY. Yeah?

SANDY. (Deadly serious, level.) ...You would have been an abortion.

(Beat. **GUY** stops cleaning her face.)

I was shamed by an entire community of women for keeping my pregnancy intact. They egged my mother's house. They painted the word SLAVE on my car. My *friends* did this. All because I wanted what was promised to me.

GUY. But... You made *choices*. And you won't take responsibility for them. You let this huge part of yourself just shrivel up –

SANDY. (Snapping.) You know what I'll take responsibility for? Diminishing you. Giving you too much privilege. Making things easy for you I'm done. Go on, go dole out some more inept blowjobs, or fall in love with some more fatties. You're free. Just let me know when you've achieved your vengeance.

(Beat.)

GUY. You have cake in your hair.

SANDY. I am aware.

GUY. How you gonna clean it?

SANDY. I don't know.

GUY. Or shower? Or feed yourself?

SANDY. I've got it covered. The monsignor will help.

(Long beat.)

GUY. I'm gonna go wait for the food.

(He exits the apartment but remains standing outside the door.)

(**SANDY** *pulls her stump-hands from the bucket. She somehow grabs some gauze and begins wrapping her hands.*)

(**GUY** *begins pacing by the door. Conflicted, stymied.*)

GUY. You're enabling her, bro...not good...

(**SANDY** *hits her Bluetooth button.*)

SANDY. Call Taylor.

GUY. You affirm her insecurities and you hate yourself for it, but you never DO anything about it.

SANDY. Taylor it's Sandy, I need to cancel my brunch with Keller and Keller. Just cancel it. No, don't reschedule. Something's come up.

GUY. You're as bad as she is. Falling into step with societal expectations. Never having the courage to do what you *really* want.

SANDY. Call Kristen.

GUY. If you weren't such a pussy you'd go straight to the club, find that chick, bring her back to your place, and bang her 'til she's brain-dead.

SANDY. Hi Kristen it's Sandy, listen, I'm not gonna be able to make lunch with Harvey so could you reschedule please, thanks.

GUY. So do it. Now. Go.

(**SANDY***'s buzzer rings. She shouts to* **GUY** *through the door.*)

SANDY. Get the door, would you?

(**GUY** *doesn't move.*)

I can hear you talking to yourself. Go downstairs and pay the delivery man.

GUY. (*Through the door, with courage.*) No.

SANDY. I'm very hungry –

GUY. I gotta help you because you won't help yourself.

SANDY. What does that mean –

GUY. Goodbye, Mom.

(*He exits.*)

SANDY. I'm sorry if I was testy. I didn't sleep well.

(*No answer.*)

Hello?

(*He's gone.*)

(*Door buzzes again. Beat. **SANDY** stands to answer it. Walks with her knees pressed tightly together to keep her uterus from falling out. Presses the intercom button with her elbow.*)

Leave the food outside the door please. Apartment 12b. Thank you.

(*Walks back to her seat with difficulty. Hits the button on her Bluetooth headset.*)

Call Chloe.

Chloe it's Sandy. I need to cancel all my appointments. No no, just for the week. I have a little cough.

(*Long beat. She stares at her stump-hands.*)

Part Eight: Rooftop Bar, Again

(In the background: A billboard advertising "OMNI Wireless Service." Photo of a woman struggling to drink water and the slogan "One Month of Free Wi-Fi. So Refreshing.")

(MEREDITH is dancing awesomely, by herself. GUY shows up. Spots MEREDITH. Watches her. Gathers courage. Then:)

GUY. "Bite me."

(She ignores him. Continues dancing.)

I was hoping you'd be here.

(She continues dancing coldly. Ignores him.)

Can I buy you a drink?

(She shakes a bottle of sport water to show she is all beveraged up.)

Not boozing tonight, huh.

(She ignores him.)

Not even strapped to your thigh?

(She ignores him.)

Are you punishing me?

(Beat.)

Can I watch you?

MEREDITH. I don't give a shit what you do.

(He watches her dance. She very clearly gives a shit what he does, as evidenced by the way she is dancing.)

GUY. I've been thinking about you. A lot. I wait until my girlfriend falls asleep and then jerk off to the idea of you writhing on my couch smeared in chocolate frosting.

MEREDITH. Um okay.

GUY. I'm just being honest.

MEREDITH. Why not.

GUY. You'd think FAR less of me if I hadn't had like sort of kinky fantasies about you –

MEREDITH. So I might like, *project* I have no boundaries because I like to be in close proximity to sexy people, but that doesn't mean I'm literally *inviting* people to shit on me.

GUY. What?

MEREDITH. Chocolate frosting?

GUY. Jesus, it's not a scat fantasy! It's a cake fantasy!

MEREDITH. Same difference. I'm bigger than I look, dickhead. Bigger than the walls, the lights, your ego. I will eat you alive.

GUY. I know you will. It's what you do. And you like it more than you ever expected to. Which makes you feel shame. Right? 'M I close?

> (**MEREDITH** *stops dancing and regards him curiously. He doesn't know if he should keep talking. He does anyway.*)

(*Muddling through.*) SO, you, you like… I dunno, it's confusing! But it's okay. It's okay to want things that maybe aren't good for you. Like me. I'm bad for you. For *sure*. But you want me anyway. And like, you're not good for me either. You're like, not who I'm supposed to be with. But you *get to have me*. Because I'm brave enough! And so are you. So…let's do this.

> (**MEREDITH** *appraises him. Suddenly, she bursts into laughter.*)

MEREDITH. Hahahahahhhahahhah.

GUY. What? What?

> (*She shakes her head and keeps laughing.*)

I can't tell if you're laughing *at* me or *with* me… That's okay… You have a great laugh. Keep going…

MEREDITH. You are FUNNY!

GUY. Cool. Hahahhhahhha...

MEREDITH. You know what else is funny?

GUY. What?

MEREDITH. Salad! Salad is hilarious!!

GUY. Yeah. Hahahhhahhhhahaha.

MEREDITH. Right?

GUY. Hahahhhahhhhahaha.

MEREDITH. Are you laughing about salad?

GUY. No, uh...I'm laughing about flame-broiled steak. Hahahahhhah. And craft beer. Hahahahha! And sports cars.

MEREDITH. Oh my god, what else? Lip gloss? Tank tops?

GUY. Jockstraps! Cuban cigars! Axe body spray!!

MEREDITH. DOGS THAT SPILL RED WINE ON BEIGE CARPETS!

> *(They both keel over laughing.* **GUY** *stops laughing first, abruptly. He grabs* **MEREDITH** *and kisses her very passionately. She kisses back. It gets nasty.)*

Are you sure –

GUY. Yeah –

MEREDITH. Okay –

GUY. Alley basement bathroom sun –

MEREDITH. Carpet. Yours.

> *(Beat.)*

GUY. Okay.

> *(***MEREDITH** *turns to grab her purse. She sees the ad with the woman struggling to drink water.)*

MEREDITH. One sec.

> *(She grabs her bottle of water, opens her mouth, and squeezes a stream of water into her eye, just like the photo.* **GUY** *is confused.)*

GUY. What the hell was that?

MEREDITH. I'm just very hot. And I have trouble drinking water. Most women do. Let's go.

Part Nine: The Carpet, Again

> (**TORI** *is doing yoga on the floor of the apartment.*)

> (**MEREDITH** *and* **GUY** *enter.* **GUY***'s arm is slung around* **MEREDITH** *and they're making out.* **MEREDITH** *still clutches her water bottle.* **TORI** *stops yoga-ing.*)

GUY. Hey.

TORI. Hey.

> (**GUY** *and* **MEREDITH** *wipe their mouths sheepishly. Beat.*)

GUY. Tori, this is Meredith.

TORI. I remember her.

MEREDITH. Hi.

> (*Beat.*)

GUY. Meredith is a dancer. Tori is a student. She has a Vespa.

TORI. You brought her here to have sex?

GUY. Yeah. That cool?

TORI. Sure.

GUY. Positive? Because, you know –

TORI. No problem. I can go to a movie or something –

GUY. Don't leave. Hang out a little.

TORI. Nah.

GUY. Seriously, Tori. We want you here.

TORI. You sure?

GUY. Positive. Meredith said she wants to make you come.

MEREDITH. I did?

GUY. At the club? That first night? You said you wanted to make her come louder and harder than I ever could. And shove her up your ass without lube.

MEREDITH. Oh yeah.

GUY. Unless…

MEREDITH. No, no, I do. It's cool. I'm down.

GUY. You sure?

MEREDITH. Yeah.

GUY. Cool. What say, Tors?

> (**TORI** *is hesitant.*)

Because I don't wanna make you do something you don't wanna do.

TORI. I know.

GUY. And you've never had a problem with this sorta thing before…

TORI. I know.

GUY. So? Look, if you feel weird we could, I could. I could maybe fire up with Meredith in the bedroom, and you could pop in later…oorrrrrrr, maybe you gals could, you know. Game it on the couch for a bit, and I could watch…your call, Tors.

> (*Beat.* **TORI** *can't decide what to do.*)

Tell you what. Let's chill. Smoke a bowl, put on some tunes, jam a little. We're all on the same team here. Who needs a drink? I got vodka in the freezer…

> (*Beat. No one makes a move. Uncomfortable.*)

Or we could order nachos and watch some [Orange is the New Black *or* Handmaid's Tale *or current streamable show]* on Netflix. Whatevs. No presh.

MEREDITH. Fuck it.

> (**MEREDITH** *walks over to* **TORI** *and kisses her aggressively.* **GUY** *is relieved.*)

GUY. Okay! Cool.

> (*Lights change. The girls rip off their clothes and* **GUY** *drops his pants. Series of very porny*

threesome poses set to some porny track. All
poses are waaay over-the-top and feature
the typical awkward, uncomfortable angles
of people posing for a camera pretending to
enjoy themselves.* **MEREDITH** *appears to be
genuinely unleashed.* **TORI** *makes sure she
looks like she's into it.)*

*(This goes on for a while. At lease twelve
extended poses, some quite acrobatic, with
requisite moaning. The entire scenario ends
with* **GUY** *squirting water from* **MEREDITH**'s
bottle into **MEREDITH**'s *eye and* **TORI**'s *chin.)*

*(Then, lights change back. All three sit
crumpled on the carpet.)*

GUY. Needed that. Whooo. That was decadent! Right?

(The girls kind of nod. **TORI** *is perfectly
composed.* **MEREDITH** *is disheveled and shell-
shocked.* **GUY** *packs a bong.)*

(To **MEREDITH**.*)* You see my guitar?

MEREDITH. No.

GUY. Vintage 1972 Gibson Les Paul Deluxe Goldtop.
Gonna learn how to play it one of these days.

(He takes a big hit. Holds the smoke in.)

And those notebooks? Moleskin. Like Hemingway. Jot
down thoughts for my novel.

TORI. They're empty.

GUY. They're new. I have others.

*(Releases his smoke. Offers the bong to
MEREDITH. She refuses.* **TORI** *accepts.)*

Everyone okay?

---

*A license to produce *Women Laughing Alone With Salad* does not
include a performance license for any third-party or copyrighted music.
Licensees should create an original composition or use music in the
public domain. For further information, please see Music Use Note on
page 3.

*(TORI nods happily. MEREDITH nods
sheepishly.)*

Good.

*(GUY looks to MEREDITH, confused. She's like a
different person. Timid, small. What the fuck
just happened?)*

(Big, awkward beat.)

GUY. Um, I'm gonna go get a beer. Anyone want anything?

TORI. I'm good with water.

MEREDITH. *(Quietly.)* If you have some salad, that would be
great.

(Small beat, then:)

GUY. Right. Okay.

*(GUY disappears. Beat. TORI lights up a
cigarette.)*

TORI. Well. You certainly looked like you were having fun...

*(MEREDITH says nothing. She dresses, super
self-conscious.)*

*(TORI stares at her, appraising her body
roughly. TORI remains in her underwear.)*

I seriously don't know how you do it.

MEREDITH. Do what?

TORI. Enjoy yourself like that when there's so much of you.

MEREDITH. Um...

TORI. I mean I dig sex. Don't get me wrong. But you were
like, on a different planet. All sloppy and loud and
aggressive. It's like you have no idea what you look like.
What's your secret?

*(MEREDITH doesn't answer. She finishes
dressing and scrunches up into a ball.)*

Don't be embarrassed. It's like, awesome to not care
about what you look like. I don't know too many
girls like that. Most of my friends are guys. I don't

understand girls and their dramas. I think it's 'cause they're jealous of me. Though I hate saying that, it's dismissive and lazy.

MEREDITH. Um.

TORI. I don't want to be dismissive of you. I want to understand why he brought you here. It can't just be your huge tits. He doesn't like big girls. I mean he's never brought one home before –

MEREDITH. Maybe he was afraid of enjoying it too much.

TORI. Ha!

MEREDITH. Or of risking his social status by indulging in an *actual* person who isn't terrified of living –

TORI. You're not terrified? Look at you.

MEREDITH. I'm just cold –

TORI. You're literally *ashamed*! That's so sad! Maybe this kind of thing isn't for you. Maybe you need a more constructive outlet for your aggression.

MEREDITH. You're not my competition, okay? Guys want to be seen in public with you. But they wanna fuck me.

TORI. Congrats. But I'd rather be seen.

> *(The sky rumbles a bit. Both women look up.)*
>
> *(**GUY** returns with a large Styrofoam container of French fucking toast.)*

GUY. Here's your "salad."

> *(She opens the container.)*

MEREDITH. This is French toast.

GUY. Yeah.

MEREDITH. I asked for salad?

GUY. I thought you were joking.

TORI. No worries. I have some here.

> *(She reaches into her purse and pulls out a small take-out container of salad. Hands it to **MEREDITH** with a plastic fork.)*

It's from lunch. Couldn't finish it all.

MEREDITH. Thank you. This looks delicious. Yum.

> (**MEREDITH** *holds a forkful of salad to her mouth but does not eat.* **GUY** *is uncomfortable. He appraises* **MEREDITH**.*)*

GUY. You don't have to eat that if you don't want.

MEREDITH. Of course I want.

I love salad, obviously.

> (**TORI** *giggles.*)

GUY. What's funny?

TORI. Nothing. You.

GUY. Why? 'Cause I brought home a real woman for once?

TORI. Oh, is that what she is?

GUY. *(To* **MEREDITH**.*)* Just drop it. No one cares.

MEREDITH. *I care.* You know sometimes? When I eat salad? I'm like, *hell yeah.* I don't even need dressing. Just a tiny squeeze of lemon. And some cracked black pepper. Ha ha ha ha just the thought of cracked black pepper makes me giggle. Heee heee heee –

GUY. Then eat it.

> (**MEREDITH** *puts the fork in her mouth and chews. She looks delighted.* **GUY** *looks nauseated.* **TORI** *smiles.*)

TORI. How is it?

MEREDITH. I'll be honest with you. It's the best fucking salad I've ever eaten.

TORI. *(To* **GUY**.*)* And you thought she was different just 'cause she's a size twelve.

MEREDITH. I'm an eight.

> *(The sky rumbles a bit more.* **GUY** *is sort of crushed. He's watching her eat the salad in disbelief.)*

GUY. *(To* **MEREDITH**, *ignoring the sky.)* Unbelievable.

MEREDITH. Okay a ten, Jesus.

GUY. What is your deal, girlie? Seriously.

MEREDITH. Um that's a broad / question.

GUY. You just, you do everything and enjoy nothing? Huh? Is that nice for you? Pretending to be something you're not?

MEREDITH. She does it too!

GUY. I expect it of her. But not you.

MEREDITH. You don't know me. I'm... I *am* enjoying / it.

GUY. You are full of shit. You are both full of shit.

TORI. Me? What did I do?

> *(Small beat.)*

MEREDITH. I'm sorry –

GUY. Jesus Christ I am so sick of the apologizing –

TORI. Baby, I love you –

GUY. No, Tori. You don't. Because if you did, you wouldn't hate yourself so much.

TORI. I'm sorry –

GUY. Enough! Get out. Both of you. Now.

TORI. I'm not leaving!

MEREDITH. Well I'm not leaving!

> *(The sky rumbles again, louder than ever. It is terrifying. All look up.)*
>
> *(Then, three tons of lettuce drop from the sky, landing with an enormous, terrifying thud on the ground and the women.)*
>
> *(**TORI** and **MEREDITH** turn into animals.)*

TORI. Get out!

MEREDITH. No you get out!

> *(They attack each other mercilessly with salad, forcing one another to eat. It is a vicious battle. Goes on for a while. At first **GUY** is like, yeah, go on, kill yourselves.)*

MEREDITH.

Psycho –

GUY.

Is this what you want?

Huh? Make you feel good?
Everything better now?
Happy? You happy now?

TORI.

Hippo –

MEREDITH. Ferret-face –

TORI. Succubus –

> *(But then* **GUY** *realizes they are actually doing just that. He becomes terrified. He wants to stop it. He tries. But he doesn't know how.)*

GUY. Okay enough. Stop. Stop it. Okay stop! Stop it! Hey! Jesus! No! Oh god…

> *(He curls up into a ball and shivers in the corner.)*

> *(Finally, the women suffocate on the salad and die.)*

> *(***GUY*** observes them. Checks their pulses. Pulls wet lettuce from their mouths. He is heartbroken, in grief.)*

It's my fault…it's my fault… I killed them…

> *(Maybe he cries a little.)*

Momma…

> *(Beat.* **SANDY** *appears. She is wrapped entirely in bandages. She approaches* **GUY.** *Disgusted.)*

SANDY. Why can't you just grow the hell up and be a man?

GUY. I don't know –

> *(***SANDY*** punches him hard in the face with a stump. It hurts them both. Beat.)*

SANDY. You should have gone with the skinny one.

> *(She exits, leaving* **GUY** *alone with the two dead women and piles of lettuce.)*

ACT TWO

Part Ten: The Conference Room

(Long table. Fluorescent lights. Water bottles. Folders. PowerPoint presentation screen. A woman laughing alone with salad on the screen, next to a woman struggling to drink water. Both are similar to the images we have seen in the previous act. However, there's something more modern-looking about them. Perhaps the women are of mix ethnicity. Perhaps the salad bowls are more contemporary. Beneath both images, the slogan "Effervatol. You. Are. Here." Effervatol logo.)

(Long beat.)

*(**JOE** enters, now a man played by the woman who played Tori. He checks his computer. Turns off the slide. Turns up the lights. Sits. Checks his phone for messages. Fidgets. Places some pads around the table with pencils. Sits again. Applies lip balm. Eats some gum. Spits it out because it's gross. Chews loudly on a breath mint. He is very nervous.)*

*(Several moments later **BRUCE** comes in, now a dude played by the woman who played Meredith. He is nervous too.)*

BRUCE. Joe! Hey man, how's it going?

JOE. Bruce, what up, bro?

(They do a bro handshake. Elaborate.)

BRUCE. I'm pumped. I am pumped. Ya nervous?

JOE. Nope. Photos are on-point. Tags are tight. I think we nailed it this time.

BRUCE. I think so too, man.

JOE. Fourth time's a charm.

BRUCE. Our boy is gonna cream himself.

JOE. And now *that* image is in my head.

BRUCE. As if it wasn't already.

JOE. Yikes!

BRUCE. Zing!

JOE. Two points!

BRUCE. Saaa-wish!

(They high five. Beat.)

JOE. Okay I'm not gonna lie.

BRUCE. You are shitting yourself.

JOE. Aren't you?

BRUCE. Why would I be?

JOE. 'Cause of the last three times maybe?

BRUCE. Yeah but this time is different. You know how I know?

JOE. How?

BRUCE. I feel it in my ball sack.

JOE. For real?

BRUCE. Yup. Like someone ringing a cowbell.

JOE. Hell yeah.

(Beat. They are still nervous. They attempt to allay this.)

BRUCE. Hey, catch the game last night?

JOE. Are you kidding? Motherfucker drained a buzzer-beating three-pointer and knocked those suckers right out of first. Suh-WEEEEEET.

BRUCE. Man what a swish, right? That kid is smooth as a summer lake.

JOE. That kind of talent?

BRUCE. Fella was born to move. Physically, he's like, an education. A formal education in the fluidity of the human form.

JOE. Well said.

BRUCE. I appreciate aptitude. Freshman year we had this dude on our team? Sick motherfucker. Six foot three? Super-cut? They called him "The Candle."

JOE. "The Candle"?

BRUCE. Yeah, man. Bastard bleached his hair white and dyed the tips orange. Gelled that shit straight up. And he was Indian.

JOE. Like Native American, or –

BRUCE. No, like Tech Supportty. A wonder to behold. Like the Greeks. In Grecian times.

JOE. Peak physical form, is...you know?

BRUCE. And you're like, wait a minute. I have a body too. I could do that. If I trained.

JOE. There's no way you could do that. There's no way *I* could do that.

BRUCE. If you trained. Yes you could.

JOE. Okay what kind of training are we talking about?

BRUCE. Um rigorous?

JOE. No.

BRUCE. Daily rigorous training. Mind over matter. You're the master of your own physique.

JOE. *(Re: **BRUCE**'s gut.)* Who is? You?

BRUCE. Hey this is a choice.

JOE. Dude, all you really need is like, two hours per week of kettlebell swings.

BRUCE. Bullshit.

JOE. Yeah. Look.

> (**JOE** *makes a muscle.*)

BRUCE. Shut the front door. That's from two hours a week?

JOE. For real. It's called the ACE method. Adherence, consistency, and efficientness.

BRUCE. Where'd you read about that?

JOE. It's everywhere. Look it up.

BRUCE. I will do that.

(*Longish beat. They are more nervous.*)

Did he say he was gonna be late?

JOE. Um, his assistant sent an email around…the strategic planning thing is running over.

BRUCE. Oh. I didn't get that email.

JOE. He just sent it like a minute ago. You were probably on your way over.

BRUCE. Oh.

(*He checks his phone.*)

Yup. There it is. Cool. Chill man.

JOE. I'm totes chill.

(*Longish beat.*)

(*The men stand and begin to air-box one another casually.*)

BRUCE. Dude. You smell like smoke.

JOE. No I don't.

BRUCE. You do. You completely do.

JOE. Nah, man. I used Listerine.

BRUCE. Your clothes, brah.

JOE. You can't smell them from there.

BRUCE. I can, I totally can smell them from here.

JOE. Really? Shit.

BRUCE. Thought you quit.

JOE. So did I. Hell, keeps me from packing on the pounds…

(*He playfully pokes at **BRUCE**'s belly. **BRUCE** swats him away.*)

BRUCE. Hey. Whatever, man. I'd rather die choking on a maple-bourbon-smoked pork belly than a pair of black rotting lungs.

JOE. Choose your poison.

BRUCE. Decadence or bust. That's my jam.

JOE. Mine is smokes and my motorcycle. I love that bike. Sometimes I'll park it on the street, then sit on my stoop and watch people check it out. Hairy dudes always want to touch it.

BRUCE. Ride or die baby.

(They stop air-boxing.)

(Longish beat. They sit. Check their phones.)

JOE. They're saying two more minutes.

BRUCE. That means twenny.

JOE. Natch.

(The men drop to the floor and start doing push-ups, sit-ups, plank-punches, and other floor/wall exercises casually. Maybe they lift stuff.)

So do you like beer?

BRUCE. Love beer, yeah. I'm a beer guy.

JOE. What kind of beer would you recommend for a non-beer drinker?

BRUCE. You wanna get into the brew?

JOE. Yeah. I'm thinking I'd like to have a hobby.

BRUCE. I mean would you be down with some deeply complex oaky reds, or like a barrel-aged stout?

JOE. Um…

BRUCE. Or maybe something lighter and hoppier, like an IPA or a barley wine?

JOE. God I have no idea.

BRUCE. Tell you what. Belgians are a good place to start. It's a diverse host of styles –

JOE. Sure, sure –

BRUCE. – But maybe start by trying a Chimay Blue or Chimay Red. They're more alcoholic than average beers, and they drink more like a complex red wine –

JOE. Okay –

BRUCE. I mean we're not talking pound-a-six-pack-watching-CSI kinda thing –

JOE. No no. I want to cultivate a palate.

BRUCE. Okay cool, 'cause that's a good start. And those are good for this time of year too. In warmer weather I'd recommend an American-style wheat beer.

JOE. Cool, thanks bro.

BRUCE. Any time, bro.

> (*Longish beat. They check their phones. They are still nervous. More so.*)

JOE. Shit. He's on his way.

BRUCE. Cool. Relax. It's allllllll good.

> (*The men start jerking themselves off casually.*)

I sent Caroline to the Starbucks this morning.

JOE. Not Dunkins?

BRUCE. Nah.

JOE. But that's like, five extra blocks.

BRUCE. I know. I was in the mood to mess with her a little.

JOE. You're such a dick.

BRUCE. Look, no one told her to wear that tiny little skirt in the dead of winter. Serves her right for dressing inappropriately. I mean seriously.

JOE. Why do chicks do that to themselves? Self-loathing, or –

BRUCE. Yeah, man. They're like, socialized to value appearance over comfort. Meanwhile who gives a crap?

JOE. Not me.

BRUCE. I mean come on. Wake up and smell the reverse-misogyny. No one needs to look at your tits. We've seen tits before. We need to look at your *brains*.

JOE. Seriously. I don't know one dude on this planet who'd kick a girl out of bed for not being a size zero, or not having a hairless vagina...

BRUCE. It's so they can get naked in a dressing room and have the other girls hate on them.

JOE. For once I just want to be honest. "Yes, you look like a forty-five-year-old mother of three in those jeans. But it's okay! Just lay off the salty foods for a week."

BRUCE. "You're stuffing your face with SnackWell's, which is like –"

JOE. I *hate* SnackWell's –

BRUCE. Oh they're horrible. They taste like chocolate-covered monkey dick. I'm like, don't eat seventeen low-fat cookies and then bitch about the size of your ass. Eat ONE cookie, and make it a good one, and feel okay about it after. For fuck's sake.

JOE. Seriously.

BRUCE. I mean.

JOE. Seriously.

> *(They can't finish. Too much pressure. They stop masturbating.)*
>
> *(Longish beat. **BRUCE** squirts some hand sanitizer into **JOE**'s hands.)*

Thanks, bro.

BRUCE. Any time, bro.

> *(**BRUCE** squirts some into his own hand. They rub their hands together for a while.)*
>
> *(**BRUCE** then applies lip balm. Offers some to **JOE**. **JOE** refuses.)*
>
> *(Finally **GUY** comes in the door, played by the woman who played Sandy.)*

GUY. Sorry I'm / late.

BRUCE. No worries.

JOE. We were just bro-ing out.

> *(**GUY** situates himself at the end of the table, the place of power.)*

GUY. Everyone have a good weekend?

BRUCE. S'alright. Played poker with my drinking buddies. Lost like three hundy.

GUY. Ouch.

BRUCE. Yeah, I'm not very good at it. But I'm addicted to the rush. Keep me away from Vegas, man.

GUY. No doubt.

BRUCE. And, I got some new ink.

GUY. Sweet. Where at?

BRUCE. Right below my heart. It's in Hindi. "Let them hate...as long as they fear." Ow. You got any tattoos?

GUY. *(Slightly ashamed.)* One. Skull above my pubic bone. Got it when I was fifteen. Like an idiot.

BRUCE. Sweet.

GUY. *(To* **JOE**.*)* And how was your weekend?

JOE. I went fishing with my dad over in Port Washington. He's got a little place there.

GUY. Catch anything?

JOE. A bluefish. Couple rainbow trout.

GUY. Cook 'em up? Eat 'em?

JOE. Gut 'em right there on the boat, grill them back home on our Viking.

GUY. Excellent.

JOE. What about you?

> *(Beat.)*

GUY. I buried my mother.

JOE.	**BRUCE**.
No...	Oh snap!

GUY. She was. Her body was. I mean her insides. I guess she was in denial, or. Anyway.

BRUCE. Holy shit.

JOE. I'm so sorry, bro.

BRUCE. Are you okay?

GUY. Yeah. I mean I hadn't seen her in six years. Last time I saw her she punched me in the face.

JOE.	BRUCE.
Aw HAIL to the naw –	That's harsh –

GUY. She's a passionate woman. *Was.* Um.

BRUCE. Death is messed up. She leave you anything?

GUY. Not a dime. Willed everything to an elderly priest who lives in her building. She um. She told me once she made things too easy for me. Said it diminished me.

> *(Awkward beat.)*

JOE. Sucks, man.

GUY. Yeah. So.

> *(Awkward beat.)*

Moving on. Heard you guys were workin' late Friday night.

JOE. 'Til midnight, yeah.

BRUCE. We wanted to knock it out of the park this time.

GUY. Good. 'Cause the Big Boss was breathing down my neck all last week. This New Regime does not mess around.

JOE. Damn.

BRUCE. What'd you say?

GUY. I said we needed a couple days.

JOE. How'd that go?

GUY. It didn't. We have 'til tonight.

JOE. Oh crap.

GUY. This is our asses, boys. I need to walk out of this room today with something I can show people. So. Whatcha got?

BRUCE. Jeez. All right. So um, you'll be happy to know we trashed everything from before. All our ideas from the past couple months.

JOE. The broken wind-up doll, the bummed-out animated talking blob, the woman being chased by the Robe of Sadness – all gone.

BRUCE. Those old-school pharma tactics worked for quite a while, don't get me wrong. But as you know, our sales have begun to decline. So!

> *(The boys get into "pitch mode.")*

THIS time, we did a little research on the quote/unquote –

BRUCE & JOE. "Millennial woman."

– Her wants, desires, et cetera. And here's what we found.

JOE. The –

BRUCE & JOE. "Millennial woman."

JOE. – Is not interested in defining herself by her worst features. She was raised by parents who treated her like a rare precious flower, and she believes it.

BRUCE. She is a projection of her greatest desires for herself, an amalgam of her finest qualities, and the culmination of her noblest aspirations. She is, if you pardon the hyperbolic language, a self-prescribed goddess. AND, she refuses to align herself with the image of a haggard poorly-dressed sunken-eyed gal crumpled in a corner.

JOE. "That gal is effed up."

BRUCE & JOE. Glad she isn't me.

BRUCE. My friend? THIS IS WHAT WE HAVE BEEN MISSING. We can no longer afford to be in the business of affirming the negative. If we are to move forward as a company, our job must be to help the consumer live up to an *ideal* vision of herself. And how do we do this? By giving her tools.

One tool in particular, that is…

BRUCE & JOE. Effervatol.

> *(**BRUCE** lowers the lights slightly. **JOE** taps a little on his computer. A PowerPoint presentation reveals a slide show of all the photos of women laughing alone with salad and women struggling to drink water. Superimposed on each image is the word*

"Effervatol" with a catchphrase next to it. The boys read each catchphrase on the slides with conviction and gusto.)

JOE. "Effervatol. Healthy is Happy."

(*Next slide.*)

BRUCE. "Effervatol. It's You. Only Better."

(*Next slide.*)

JOE. "Effervatol. Release Your Bliss."

(*Next slide.*)

BRUCE. "Effervatol. We Got You, Girl."

(*Next slide.*)

JOE. "Effervatol. A Spa Day. In a Pill."

(*Next slide.*)

BRUCE. "Effervatol. Nothing Tastes as Good as Happy Feels."

(*Next slide.*)

JOE. "Effervatol. You Can Totally Fix This."

(*Next slide.*)

BRUCE. "Effervatol. It's Not Them. It's You."

(*Next slide.*)

JOE. "Effervatol. Better Than Brunch."

(*Next slide.*)

BRUCE. "Effervatol. Fewer Calories Than Midol."

(*Next slide.*)

JOE. "Effervatol. When Life Hands You Lululemon."

(*Next slide.*)

BRUCE. "Effervatol. No More Crying at Work."

(*Next slide.*)

JOE. "Effervatol. He's Just Not That Into Moods."

(*Next slide.*)

BRUCE. "Effervatol. Exfoliate Your Mind."

(Next slide.)

JOE. "Effervatol. Swipe Right on Life."

(Next slide.)

BRUCE. "Effervatol. For When You Can't Even."

(Next slide.)

JOE. "Effervatol. Shawty, You Feel Me?"

(Next slide.)

BRUCE. "Effervatol. It Texts You Back."

(Next slide.)

JOE. "Effervatol. Because You *Should* Smile More."

(Next slide.)

BRUCE. "Effervatol. You Like Orgasms, Right?"

(Next slide.)

JOE. "Effervatol. Because Yorkies Die."

BRUCE. And my favorite, although it's a bit abstract...

(Next slide. It's the slide from the top of the act.)

"Effervatol. You. Are. Here."

*(Beat. **BRUCE** lets this last image sit a while. Then he turns the lights up again.)*

Well. That's what we have so far. Um.

*(Big beat as **GUY** considers. **BRUCE** sits back down and begins immediately fidgeting with his pencil. **JOE** closes his computer.)*

Um.

What, ah...

Whattaya think?

*(Bigger beat. **GUY** smiles a little.)*

*(Lights change to some sort of special on **GUY**. He addresses us directly. **JOE** and **BRUCE** don't hear this...they fidget as if they're still waiting*

for a response. Or they freeze. Whatever
works. But this should feel like a completely
different plane of reality.)

GUY. So...my mother punches me in the face with a bloody
stump. A week later, I decide to grow the hell up and
be a man. I send out résumés. I secure an entry-level
position in a big corporation. I sit down at a desk and
close my eyes. And when I open them, six years have
passed. Like nothing. They just pass. And in my head
I'm like, how is that even possible? When all I ever
wanted was to care enough to beat the crap out of
something? Or smash a guitar, or pound beers like a
caveman, or tear the sleeves off my shirt WHILE I'M
WEARING IT, or any of that other shit...because *I*
wanted what was promised to me. But when I open my
eyes, it's six years later and I'm a department head at a
pharmaceutical company. Marketing. And my mother
is dead.

(Long beat.)

After the funeral, the monsignor and I take the limo
back to her apartment. The first place I find myself
is her fridge. Ketchup, vodka, frozen peas. Like a
bachelor. And of course. Four bulk plastic sacks of pre-
washed certified-organic herbed greens.

Then her bathroom. Endless rows of prescription
bottles. Beauty products piled four and five deep on her
giant vanity sink. An altar to self-preservation in the
church of Gonna-Fucking-Die.

But instead. I leave the bathroom and walk over to the
hutch. Her photo albums are sitting there like a middle
finger flipping me off.

I open the oldest one first.

1972. Short pixie cut. Striped tank. Round sunnies.
Holding her purse in one hand, a sign in the other. "MY
BODY – MY CHOICE." She isn't smiling. None of the
women are smiling. Some of them are screaming. She
isn't, though. She's just. She's standing. Getting her
photo taken.

She's fourteen.

Um.

So I start to panic. In my head I'm like, this isn't happening. None of it. THIS IS A DREAM. I'm dreaming I'm a mid-level exec in my thirties. I dream I'm surrounded by douchebags. In my dream the douchebags are prep-school boys. The younger one's parents are therapists. The older one minored in Women's Studies. They are promising, bright, attractive imbeciles. And they're right. About everything. And they don't feel one ounce of shame over it.

And I wonder if I really *am* a coward and a loser. Because if I had wanted to tear off my sleeves so bad, maybe I wouldn't have put a down-payment on a condo in Williamsburg or started collecting antique string instruments. Or maybe I would have tried a little harder to stop becoming the thing I loathe. Because in my dream. I have become the thing I loathe. It bothers me, but in my dream I say, it's okay, this happens to everyone.

Because I have become the thing I loathe. It bothers me but it's okay, this happens to everyone.

Because I have become the thing I loathe. And it is humiliating.

   (Beat.)

And I'm staring at that screen and suddenly, I have the sensation I'm pedaling on a bicycle across the Manhattan Bridge at sunset, and the road tips down and my dirty city feet fly from the pedals and the pedals spin-spin-spin and the sky goes black and the bridge disappears and all I feel is the terror of not stopping and the summer wind is too hot against my skin and I'm getting burned, I'm blistering, and images flash against my eyelids, Tori over a toilet, Meredith covered in cake, and I scream at the wind, I beg it to tell me the story of the women who haunt me and it screams back,

"No asshole, figure it out!" And I scream, "How??!! I don't fucking know how!"

And at this moment. I understand two things.

One. This is not a dream. It's an exaggerated reality. It sucks.

And two? I am about to walk into my boss's office. And let my feet fly off the pedals.

'Cause I'm done feeling ashamed.

Part Eleven: The Corner Office

(A lush corner office. Well-appointed desk.)

*(The actor who played Guy in Act One is now playing **ALICE**, C.E.O. of the pharma company. She is seated behind a desk. She wears a feminine, tasteful ensemble. She is pleasant, attractive, in control.)*

*(**GUY** walks in, agitated. He grips a portfolio. Places it on Alice's desk.)*

GUY. Okay so, before you peruse these images, let me just say this:

As you may know

I've been at this company for six years.

This campaign is.

It's different.

It's provocative.

And I'm certainly in a position to judge.

I have a creative writing degree.

I've had a sexual encounter with a man.

I collect vintage guitars.

I've had an ulcer since I was / twenty.

ALICE. I've already looked at them.

GUY. You did?

ALICE. On my lunch. I understand you'd prefer to walk me through them, but I don't have a lot of time. It's my assistant Jordan's birthday, they're doing a little thing for him any minute. Also I have to feed Juliet.

> *(**ALICE** gestures to the baby monitor on her desk.)*

GUY. It's so great having her here, isn't it?

ALICE. It is. Though I've been getting some flack in the press for putting in the nursery. Especially from women. But my focus is so much sharper with her on-site. Plus I can work longer hours.

GUY. It takes a lot of courage, doing something like that after only having been here a couple months.

ALICE. I'm happy with the decision.
In general I have a hard time feeling shame for the things I want.

>   *(Beat.)*

So.
Let's chat briefly.
Effervatol.
Haven't we seen these images before?

GUY. Similar ones, perhaps. But not used to market pills. And, we've updated them considerably. We used a brand-new cutting-edge stock photography database to find photos that speak directly to our contemporary culture. Instead of iceberg lettuce, we've used *exotic greens*. Kale, frisée, watercress, et cetera. We included women of *indeterminate* backgrounds. Mixed race, if you will. And finally, and perhaps most radically, we've moved *out of the kitchen*. We're covering *all* areas of the home. Living room, bedroom, basement –

ALICE. Why salad?

GUY. Well to our capitalist neoliberal society, salad imagery represents self-control and status. And there's a subtextual shaming going on as well, of course. Women respond incredibly well to this sort of reinforcement, studies show. These images are very representative.

ALICE. Of what?

GUY. The Idealized Modern Female.

ALICE. Meaning...

GUY. Healthy, active, slender, bright, positive, energetic, self-possessed, relaxed, sexy, confident, gorgeous, independent, accomplished, intelligent, empathetic, well-read, honest, maternal, youthful, chaste, endearing, funny, fun-loving, lucid, um, feminine, athletic, charming, benevolent, kind, educated, outgoing, engaged, present, concerned, intuitive, thoughtful, flexible, hilarious, um, communicative, warm, approachable, compassionate, and wise. So. Oh but also, and this is pretty huge...*non-threatening*. Our consumer doesn't want to hate these women. Our consumer wants to *be* these women. It's aspirational.

(Longish beat.)

I like that dress –

ALICE. You do know where I come from, don't you?

GUY. You mean like, regionally?

ALICE. I mean, philosophically.

GUY. Well you're a woman in a powerful position, so. You value hard work –

> (**ALICE** *moves to the front of the desk and perches on the corner.*)

ALICE. I graduated with honors from Stanford University with a BS in symbolic systems, an MBA in finance, and a PhD in immunology.

GUY. Oh / wow.

ALICE. I have a JD from Yale Law, an MFA from RISD, and an honorary degree from Trenton State in experimental theology. They recruited me from a Fortune 100 company at which I was making seven figures. And here I am, delivering my résumé to you to prove a point. Do you know why they hired me?

GUY. To change the face of the company. Make our brand appear more relevant –

ALICE. "Appear."

GUY. Poor choice of words –

ALICE. My job. Is to make sure our sales are healthy and our brand is represented in a way that feels fresh, modern, and above all, *responsible*. Because we have not done this in the past. And we are on the verge of being crippled by it.

GUY. Well I would argue our sales are down because we haven't yet found our way into the mind of our *present-day* female consumer.

ALICE. So in your opinion, these images will sell pills.

GUY. Absolutely.

ALICE. And do you also believe they are responsible?

GUY. I mean.

How do you define responsible?

ALICE. How do *you* define responsible?

(*Beat.*)

GUY. Okay look. I'm as frustrated as you are that women hate themselves. It's bullshit. I'd love to be able to change that. I'd love to be quote/unquote *responsible*. But it's so much bigger than me. And I'm tired of feeling like I should be held accountable for something that's not my fault. Because where do I even start? Should I go rip the burkas off women in the Middle East and demand they walk five paces *in front* of their husbands? Or stop bullets from entering the skulls of teenage girls who just want an education? Or call the cops on behalf of every woman who's ever been sexually harassed in the history of the universe? No. The *sole reason* I am here at this company in this job is to sell drugs to depressed women who cannot cope with the fact that the world sucks for them. And this campaign will do that. Without a doubt. Now if you have a better idea, let's talk. 'Cause I'm just about tapped.

(*A baby's laugh/gurgle is heard on the monitor.* **ALICE** *turns the volume down.*)

ALICE. Do you have any daughters?

GUY. No. No children.

ALICE. What about a girlfriend?

GUY. Nope.

ALICE. Come on. Attractive successful fella like you?

GUY. What are you asking?

(**ALICE** *moves her chair closer to* **GUY**.)

ALICE. I inherited you and your team. You've all been very polite, but we've never had a meaningful conversation.

I'd like to know where you're coming from. *Philosophically*. Assess your point of view on things.

GUY. "Things."

ALICE. Women.

    (Beat. **GUY** *is touched and surprised.)*

GUY. No one's ever asked me for that before.

ALICE. I'm sorry.

    (Beat.)

Something's on your mind. I can tell.

    *(***GUY*** says nothing.)*

Something you can't talk to me about?

GUY. No. You're my boss.

ALICE. Why not try?

    (Beat. **GUY** *pulls his chair closer as well.)*

GUY. I need answers. Lots of 'em.

ALICE. About what?

GUY. The women who haunt me.

ALICE. Who are they?

GUY. Okay. Tori. Piece of work. Always trying to be a better version of herself. It ended horribly. I told her to take her bike and get out. She threw up on her legs. Then apologized and cleaned up the floor. Moved to LA.

ALICE. Who else?

GUY. This girl I met at a club. God, her smell... Like poison and promise and promiscuity and all that other devious shit.

ALICE. This makes you angry.

GUY. Yes! At her! For having power over me.

ALICE. Okay.

GUY. Or for not *realizing* she has power. Or for realizing it and being scared of it. Or.

    (Beat.)

ALICE. And your mother?

GUY. What about her?

ALICE. You tell me.

>(*Thinks. Takes out the picture. Hands it to* **ALICE**.)

GUY. She was an activist.

>(**ALICE** *demonstratively does not take the picture.*)

ALICE. What else?

GUY. She was a cunt.

ALICE. What else?

>(*Beat.*)

GUY. How do you do it? You've managed to avoid getting taken down by the gargantuan load of bullshit that plagues normal chicks.

ALICE. (*Getting it.*) Ah. You think I can show you how to empathize with women more effectively.

GUY. Maybe?

ALICE. Which will make you feel less dead inside.

GUY. Maybe?

ALICE. And help you not experience shame.

GUY. Man, that would be great.

ALICE. (*Mic drop.*) And you'll become a better human. Because of me. Which means you don't see me as a person. You see me as a function. The function being: to serve you. I bet those "women who haunt you" have something to say about that…

>(*Long beat as* **GUY** *understands finally what she's saying.* **ALICE** *pushes the portfolio toward* **GUY**.)

What would your "activist-cunt" mother say about these images?

>(**GUY** *takes the portfolio. Considers the images. Thinks.*)

GUY. She'd say:

"Look at that psycho anorexic ferret-looking yoga bitch. I bet she'd make a great wife."
And then she'd buy some pills.

> (*Beat. He drops his head into his hands.*)

Oh my god I'm tired, Alice. I'm so tired of being...

> (*Searching...he gets there...*)

> *Here.*

ALICE. Where would you like to be?

> (*Small beat.*)

GUY. Paris.

> (**ALICE** *leans into* **GUY**.)

ALICE. (*Quietly.*) I'm going to do something for you right now.
And that will be the last thing I ever do for you.
Okay?

> (**GUY** *nods.* **ALICE** *stands. Begins to show* **GUY** *the door.*)

It's been a pleasure working with you these past few months. Someone will escort you to HR, after which you may gather / your belongings from your work area

> (**GUY** *goes berserk. Smashes a guitar. Does push-ups. Drinks four craft beers. Punches a wall. Punches himself. Drinks more beer. Lifts some weights. Tears the sleeves off his shirt. Does something with flame-broiled steak, craft beer, sports cars, jockstraps, Cuban cigars, and Axe body spray. Roars like a lion. Not necessarily in that order.*)

> (**ALICE** *watches this all very calmly.*)

> (*Then he's done. Beat as he catches his breath.* **JOE** *knocks on the door tentatively.*)

JOE. S'cuse me...they're doin' the cake now, so...

(Beat. **JOE** *realizes he's walked into something uncomfortable.)*

Sorry.

*(***JOE*** *exits.)*

ALICE. We good?

*(***GUY*** *says nothing.* **ALICE** *exits.)*

*(***GUY*** *is left alone on the stage.)*

(Beat.)

(Voices from offstage can be heard singing:)

VOICES. *(Offstage.)*
HAPPY BIRTHDAY TO YOU
HAPPY BIRTHDAY TO YOU
HAPPY BIRTHDAY DEAR JORDAN
HAPPY BIRTHDAY TO YOU!

(A lone lettuce leaf flutters from the sky and lands at **GUY**'s *feet.)*

(He picks it up and stares at it.)

VOICE. *(Offstage.)* Who wants a slice of cake?

(Blackout.)

End of Play

9 780573 707650